For Ans Hey

First published in the United States, Great Britain, Canada, Australia, and New Zealand in 2011
by North-South Books Inc., an imprint of NordSüd Verlag AG, CH-8005 Zürich, Switzerland.
Distributed in the United States by North-South Books Inc., New York 10017.

Library of Congress Cataloging-in-Publication Data is available.
Printed in Germany by Grafisches Centrum Cuno GmbH & Co. KG, 39240 Calbe, June 2011.
ISBN: 978-0-7358-4030-0 (trade edition)
1 3 5 7 9 • 10 8 6 4 2

www.northsouth.com

FSC
www.fsc.org
MIX
Paper from
responsible sources
FSC® C043106

Hans de Beer

LITTLE POLAR BEAR

Little Polar Bear and the Submarine

NorthSouth
New York / London

Lars, the little polar bear, lived at the North Pole in the middle of snow and ice. He was a very curious little bear, so every day he went out to explore.

"Watch where you step," Mother warned him. "The ice is melting very fast this year. If you're not careful, you could be carried away on an ice floe."

Mother was right. The snow had already melted in a lot of places, and the ice was breaking up. Lars didn't think that was all bad, though. It was fun to splash around in the warm water, and he loved to sunbathe too.

But playing in the snow was still the most fun for a little polar bear, and fortunately there was still enough snow up on the hills.

If only there was someone to play with—playing all by himself got boring. As it had grown warmer, Lars's friends and their families had moved farther north where there was still plenty of snow and ice.

Feeling a little sad, Lars started back home. Then he spotted some footprints. They were still fresh! Whose footprints could they be?

Curious, Lars followed the tracks. Maybe it was someone he could play with.

The tracks led down the hillside to the bay, where a big black monster was floating in the water. The monster was making loud booming noises, and smoke puffed out of its belly.

"Well, how about that!" said a strange voice. "We don't see a single polar bear for weeks, and now we see three cubs in just a couple of days."

"Who are *you*?" said Lars. There in front of him was a very long dog with very short legs.

"I'm Freddy the dachshund," said the dog. Then he added proudly, "I'm the ship's dog, from that submarine over there."

"Oh . . . hello, . . . I'm Lars," said Lars shyly. "Why did you say *three* cubs?"

"I'll tell you why," said Freddy. "As you've probably noticed, it's unusually warm here this year." Lars nodded. "Every year there's less snow and ice at the North Pole," Freddy continued. "My owners came here in their research submarine to find out just how much ice has melted.

"We've been traveling for weeks. Every day we come up to the surface to measure the ice. A couple of days ago we found two polar bear cubs on an ice floe, floating all alone on the sea. They're too young to swim. My owners rescued them."

"They have to get back to their parents!" cried Lars.

"But we don't know where they live," said Freddy.

"I'll take them!" said Lars confidently. "I've been lost lots of times, and I've always found my way back home. I know exactly what to do."

"Okay," said Freddy. "I'll get you aboard."

So after dark Freddy smuggled Lars onto the big submarine.

"Shhh," whispered Freddy. "Can't you be quieter?"

Lars was amazed. There were pipes and gauges all over the submarine.

Freddy led the way through the dimly lit passageways. "We have to be careful," he whispered. "If my owners see you, they might want to rescue you too and keep you on board. We need to hurry."

"The cubs are here in the captain's cabin," said Freddy.

Two pairs of eyes looked curiously at Lars.

"Hello, little ones," Freddy whispered. "This is Lars. He's going to take you home."

"I'm Nina," said one of the cubs.

"And I'm Nonni," said the other. "Nina's brother. Are you really going to take us home?"

"Absolutely!" Lars promised.

Suddenly a bell rang.

"We're diving again!" cried Freddy nervously. "Lars, you have to hide until we resurface. Make sure no one sees you."

A friendly scientist brought Freddy and the baby cubs something to eat. They begged for more until they had enough for Lars too.

The little cubs were so happy to have Lars there, and Lars liked being
the big bear that the young ones looked up to.

"Please, Lars, tell us another of your adventures," begged Nonni. Lars
told them stories until they all fell asleep.

The next day Freddy came to get them. The submarine had surfaced
again.

"Hurry!" Freddy whispered. "This way. The hatch is open. Let's get you
out of here!"

"Put on your swim belts and stay close to Lars," said Freddy.

"Don't worry," said Lars. "It's not far to shore, and there are lots of ice floes. We won't have any trouble making it."

Freddy waved one last time, and the hatch closed. Then the big tower of the submarine slipped slowly under the water.

All alone in the middle of the sea, Lars began to feel like a baby himself, but he didn't let it show.

"See!" Lars laughed with relief as he pushed the ice floe quickly toward shore. "Everything's going smoothly."

"Aye, aye, Captain!" said Nina and Nonni.

At last they reached land, but unfortunately Captain Lars had no idea where they were.

"Uh . . . why don't you keep your swim belts on for now," he said as calmly as he could.

If only he knew which direction to take. And to make matters worse, it was starting to snow. Nina and Nonni were beginning to get frightened.

There was nothing to do but start walking. The three friends fought their way through the snowstorm.

"We should have stayed with Freddy," Nina whined, and Nonni started to cry.

"Hang in there, kids," said Lars. "We're bound to get there soon." He tried to cheer up the cubs, but he was exhausted himself and really didn't know what to do next.

They found a place under a big rock to spend the night. Then they cuddled up close to one another and, tired out, fell asleep instantly.

It was morning when Lars awoke. An arctic fox was standing right in front of him.

"You're lost, aren't you?" said the fox.

"No . . . uh . . . well, sort of," said Lars, embarrassed. "That is, I know where we want to go. I just don't know how to get there."

"Well, it's your lucky day," said the fox. "We arctic foxes just happen to have the best noses in the north." He sniffed the two cubs. Then he sniffed Lars.

"Got it!" he announced. "These two little ones come from far away."

"What about me?" asked Lars.

"Not you," said the fox. "I can take you back to *your* home. Easy."

The four of them set off. Nina and Nonni were in good spirits again, and it wasn't long before Lars began to recognize his surroundings. Soon he was happily introducing the cubs to his parents.

"Mom, Dad, this is Nina, and that's Nonni."

"How do you do," said the cubs politely.

Lars told his parents all about Freddy and the submarine and their adventurous journey home. Mother gave Nina and Nonni a big cuddle. Father proudly patted his son on the back and thanked the arctic fox for bringing the three of them home safe and sound. Then the fox told them exactly where the two young cubs lived.

"That's much too far to take you before winter sets in." Mother smiled. "Nina and Nonni will just have to stay with us until spring."

"But then Lars and I will take you back to your parents," Father promised.

"Great!" Lars laughed. "Then I'll have all winter to teach you two how to swim! Let's get started right now!"

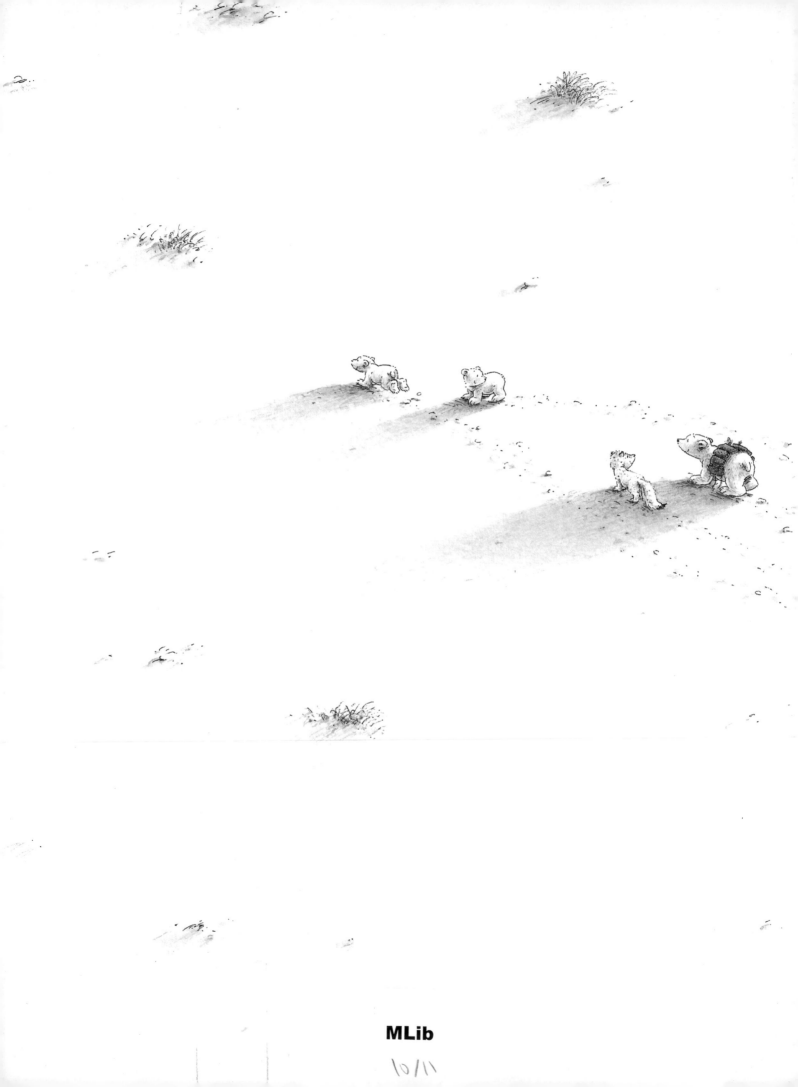